# SMALL SOLDIERS

## THE JUNIOR NOVELIZATION

# SMALL SOLDIERS

## THE JUNIOR NOVELIZATION

BY GAVIN SCOTT
BASED UPON THE SCREENPLAY WRITTEN BY
GAVIN SCOTT AND ADAM RIFKIN AND
TED ELLIOTT & TERRY ROSSIO

DreamWorks ™

# CHAPTER 1

Irwin Wayfair, toy designer, pressed his forehead against the cool glass window of the high-rise office building he worked in. He watched dejectedly as a crane lowered a sign into place outside. It read: HEARTLAND PLAY SYSTEMS, A DIVISION OF GLOBOTECH.

Until the week before, Irwin had worked for a company called simply Heartland *Toys*—but then the giant Globotech corporation had taken it over and added it to all the other companies they ran, from oil refineries to weapons plants. Today was the day Irwin was due to meet his new boss, the awe-inspiring Mr. Gil Mars, President of Globotech. He could hardly bear to think about it.

What if Mr. Mars didn't like the line of monster action figures Irwin had been working on for the past year? What if he said Heartland wasn't going to produce Irwin's beloved Gorgonites? Irwin had put his heart and soul into the development of these toys.

"Irwin! Come on!" said a voice behind him. Irwin turned around. It was Larry Benson, his smooth-talking, well-groomed co-worker.

"He's here?" Irwin asked with a gulp.

"On his way in," replied Larry, striding toward the boardroom. Irwin had no choice but to hurry after him, clutching a battered-looking box. Larry, of course, had a fancy custom-made display case for *his* line of toys.

"Pretty exciting, huh?" Larry said over his shoulder.

"It's kind of sad," replied Irwin. "Heartland Toys has a hundred-year tradition of bringing joy to kids. He's gonna want profits. It sucks."

Larry smirked. "Welcome to Earth, Irwin. I know our customs must seem strange to you, but that's how things work in the real world."

Irwin shook his head stubbornly. "The real world sucks," he said.

An attractive woman in a business suit and glasses was waiting for them outside the boardroom.

"Gentlemen, I'm Ms. Kegel," she said, "executive assistant to Mr. Mars. Let me be the first to welcome you to the Globotech family." She led them inside. "Just as he's done with his computer, electronics, telecommunications, munitions, chemical, and food divisions, Mr. Mars intends to bring his personal touch to Heartland Play Systems."

The boardroom was a vast space filled with polished wood and video screens showing Globotech's activities all over the world, from growing rubber trees to making tanks. Irwin looked around. There were no other people. "Are we waiting for everybody else?" Irwin asked.

"There is no longer any 'everybody else,'" Ms. Kegel replied. Irwin gulped. So it was true—Gil Mars had fired them all. And there was a good chance he'd fire Irwin and Larry, too, unless they really knocked his socks off today.

The door opened. Gil Mars, wearing an immaculate suit, strode in. "Good morning, gentlemen. I'm Gil Mars," he said. "From now on, you work for me."

Larry stepped forward to shake his new boss's hand. "Mr. Mars, it's a pleasure to meet you," he gushed. "I'm Larry Benson, and I'd just like to say how much I've admired . . ."

Gil Mars ignored Larry's outstretched hand and cut him off. "Don't bother, pal," he said. "Two minutes after I leave here I won't remember your name." He slapped one of Larry and Irwin's creations, Flatchoo of the Belch Brigade, down on the table. "Now—I believe that you guys are responsible for—this."

Irwin and Larry exchanged a nervous glance. As usual, Larry was ready, willing, and able to pass the blame on to Irwin. "The line was really Irwin's idea . . ." he began.

Mars squeezed the monster's stomach. It let out a deep, satisfied belch, and Mars laughed in delight. Larry instantly changed his tune. ". . . but once I refined the concept and created the marketing campaign, it became the single most successful product in the history of Heartland Toys."

Mars nodded. "And that's the reason you two are still on board. But now . . . What do you say we talk about the future?"

Larry gave Irwin the chance to lead off. He knew that Irwin would make a mess of his presentation and make him, Larry, look good in comparison. He was talented at that kind of strategizing. He smiled serenely as Irwin scrambled around trying to get his portfolio open, finally managing to find a figure with a face like a bulldog's, a chest like a wrestler's, legs covered in scales, and a bow and arrow slung over his shoulder. "These are the Gorgonites," Irwin began nervously. "This one's Archer, their noble captain."

Irwin spread the rest of the pictures out on the table. Among them were Ocula, who was an eye on three legs, and Slamfist, who looked like the Hunchback of Notre Dame—but uglier. He carried a rock in one hand and a massive club in the other.

Irwin looked up at Mr. Mars for encouragement. Mars said nothing. Irwin licked his lips nervously.

"The idea is, see, they're lost in our world, and they want to get home to the Land of Gorgon. So they have to find out as much about our world as possible, so they get kids to do research and investigate all kinds of stuff and . . . learn." Irwin pulled out another drawing. "And this one's Troglokhan. He's the . . ."

"Stop! Stop!" Mars shouted. "I hate it! Next!"

Irwin's face fell. He had lost the battle. The Gorgonites would never be produced by Heartland Play Systems now. Mars turned to Larry and raised an eyebrow. It was his turn.

Larry didn't bother with illustrations. His high-tech presentation put Irwin's to shame. A ruggedly handsome, buff-as-can-be soldier stood in front of a crumbling brick wall.

"Major Chip Hazard," said Larry. "Leader of the

Commando Elite!" He turned to Irwin and smirked. "Multimedia, Irwin. Look into it."

"A new age has dawned . . . for action," boomed a deep announcer's voice. "Never before have you seen a soldier like . . ."

". . . Major Chip Hazard, reporting for duty!" said the soldier, smashing his way out of his box.

The voice-over continued. "The future is here! A new dimension in high-tech fun . . ."

"Hold it! Hold on!" Mars yelled. He was interested at last. "Do they really do that?" he asked.

"Uh, no. There's a disclaimer," said Larry.

"But what if they could?" Mars said.

Larry and Irwin looked at him blankly.

Mars continued. "What I'm saying is that these toys should be the most advanced toys the consumer has ever seen. What I'm saying is that when kids play with these toys, they're so smart they play back. In short, gentlemen, I want toys that work the way they do in that commercial!"

"Uh, well, it's an interesting idea," Irwin said, trying to be polite. But Larry knew how to react when his boss came up with an idea, however ridiculous it might be.

"It's great!" he gushed. He thought for a moment. "Hey—what do you think of this for a slogan? 'The Commando Elite. Anything else is just a toy.'"

"No!" said Mars. "'The Commando Elite. *Everything* else is just a toy.'"

"Great," said Larry, not sure what the difference was.

"Sir—what you're asking for—that kind of computing power doesn't seem feasible," said Irwin.

"Irwin, listen, you take care of the software, okay?" said Larry. "We're part of Globotech now. I'm sure I can hunt up the technology."

"Darn right!' said Mars. He snapped his fingers. "Oh yeah! They're soldiers, right? And what do soldiers need?"

Larry and Irwin didn't know.

Ms. Kegel spoke up. "Enemies."

"Enemies," agreed Mars. He pointed to the Gorgonite sketches. "These monsters, these things are so ugly. So hideous. So relentlessly rotten that our soldiers have to seek them out and vaporize them!"

Irwin began to panic. This was all wrong! He had to say something. "But—that's not—sir, don't you think that's a little violent?"

"Yes!" chortled Mars. He held up Flatchoo and burped him loudly. "If there's one thing kids love more than disgusting bodily noises, it's violence."

"We call it action," said Larry. "It's more toyetic."

Irwin was still not convinced. "Well, I'm not sure," he said.

Mars stared at him. "What's the problem?" he asked. "They're just *toys*."

# CHAPTER 2

The sound of the ringing bell echoed down the halls of Winslow Corners High School. Students spilled out of classrooms and swarmed to their lockers, laughing and shouting. It was the final bell of the day. Even better, it was Friday.

Alan Abernathy stood alone at the bike rack, opening his combination lock. He was in a rush—he had places to go, things to do. Out of nowhere, a loafered foot appeared on the rack next to him. Alan looked up—and into the face of Mr. Florens, Winslow High's principal. He did not look happy. Alan took a closer look. No, he was definitely not happy at all. His shirt and tie were soaking wet. Alan saw his own face reflected in Mr. Florens's mirrored sunglasses and stifled a smile.

"Hello, Abernathy," the principal said.

Alan didn't say a word.

"Seems someone put gum in the nozzle of the faculty drinking fountain," Mr. Florens continued. "Do you have something you want to tell me?"

"Good luck in the wet T-shirt contest?" said Alan.

Mr. Florens's eyes narrowed. " This is the same kind of stunt that bought you trouble at your old school," he said. And then added, for effect, "Your old *schools*."

Alan took a quick look around. A crowd of onlookers had gathered, including Christy Fimple, the best-looking freshman in the whole place. Alan gave her a glance, then looked away.

"Reread my transcripts," said Alan. "I'm a little more original than that."

Mr. Florens scowled. "I don't like original, Abernathy. And I don't like troublemakers—not on my watch." He gave Alan one final glare, then stalked off.

Embarrassed, Alan sighed, pulled his bike out of the rack, and pedaled off.

Fifteen minutes later he was cycling down a narrow street in the center of the small town of

Winslow Corners. He was headed toward a tiny store called The Inner Child. It was owned by Alan's dad, Stuart. The Abernathy family had moved from Chicago a few months before to find "the quiet life." The store was certainly quiet enough—it never had any customers.

As he went into the cozy, musty interior, Alan looked at the familiar shelves full of puzzles, hand-crafted dolls, and—his father's pride and joy—intricate wooden boat models, and shook his head. No wonder there were never any kids in the store. There were no war toys, no soldiers, no squirt guns or action figures—none of the kinds of things kids actually wanted. Stuart Abernathy didn't believe in them.

Soft music was playing on the radio, but Stuart was anything but relaxed. "Alan, where have you been?" he exclaimed. "I still have to pack and get to the airport. I thought you'd flaked on me."

Alan rolled his eyes. "Dad, I kinda had to wait for school to finish," he said.

Stuart rushed around the store, nervously straightening things that didn't need to be straightened. He grabbed his jacket, rearranged a shelf, readjusted a boat model.

"I left a list of instructions," he said. "Make sure you lock the doors, front and back. Sometimes the register drawer sticks, so you have to jiggle it." He paused by the front door. "Oh, right—I want to jazz up the front window display. I'm thinking: Parcheesi."

"Yeah, that'll bring in the cool crowd," said Alan.

"Alan, this is serious," said Stuart. "I want to be able to trust you here."

Alan knew when to stop kidding. "I know, Dad. Don't worry," he said.

The door closed behind his father, and Alan heaved a sigh of relief. He had the store to himself at last.

# CHAPTER

# 3

Alan changed the radio station to some decent music and cranked up the volume. He flipped open a motorcycle magazine and started carefully examining an advertisement for a Honda motor scooter. He was trying to work out how many years it would take him to save up the money to buy it. The math seemed to suggest he'd be about as old as his grandfather by the time he could afford it.

His thoughts were interrupted by the sound of a truck rounding the corner into the alley next to The Inner Child. His face lit up as he recognized the sound of the engine. It was Joe's truck. Joe was the deliveryman for Heartland. Alan decided to go help him unload.

Big mistake.

"So where's your dad?" Joe asked. "I got his order here."

"He's going out of town tonight, to some seminar. I had to come straight here after school."

Joe looked surprised. "Wait a minute. He left *you* in charge?"

Alan shrugged. "Hey, it surprised me, too. I don't know if he's finally starting to trust me or if he just didn't have any choice."

Joe started handing Alan boxes. "So what's the seminar your dad's going to?"

Alan gave a rueful grin. "'How to Make a Success of Your Small Business,'" he said. If anybody needed advice on this, his father did. "My suggestion was, torch the place."

"Not a good idea," said Joe. "Arson forensics are pretty sophisticated nowadays."

Just then Alan noticed the truck was filled with dozens of boxes. "'Gorgonites.' 'Commando Elite.' What are those?"

"Let's take a look," said Joe.

Inside the store Joe opened one of the Small

Soldiers boxes, removed a tough-looking plastic soldier, and set him on the counter. "Ten-hut!" Joe said. The light on the soldier's belt buckle clicked on.

"Major Chip Hazard, mission ready and good to go, sir!" said the toy, saluting smartly.

Alan was impressed. Major Chip Hazard was kind of ridiculous, but there was something impressive about him. Alan opened another box labeled "Arch-Fiend," and took out a dorky-looking monster with a bow and arrow.

"Greetings," said the monster, "I am Archer, emissary of the Gorgonites."

Alan laughed. "He's awfully polite for a monster."

But he knew something about both the Commando Elite and the Gorgonites—unlike his father's beautiful wooden boats, *these* toys would sell.

"So Joe," Alan said. "Is there any way you could front me a set? Just say they were damaged in shipping?"

"Kid, in the trucking business we call that stealing," said Joe.

"I'll pay you back after I sell them," pleaded Alan.

Joe looked doubtful. "What about your dad's 'no war toys' policy? I can't even get him to stock Battleship."

"Don't worry about my dad. By the time he's back, they'll all be sold. And this place will have made a little money for once."

"It's that bad, huh?" asked Joe sympathetically.

"We're excited when shoplifters come in," said Alan.

Joe thought for a minute. "Okay, one set," he said at last. "I'll lose some paperwork for a while. But this had better not come back and bite me in the butt."

"It won't. I swear," said Alan.

"And *you* have to get 'em off the back of the truck," said Joe.

By the time he got the last carton into the store, Alan wasn't thinking about the toys at all. He was looking out the window at a girl getting off a motor scooter. It was Christy Fimple! Alan stared as her tousle-haired little brother, Tim, jumped off the back of the scooter and they both came inside.

"I wanted to go to Toy World!" Tim whined.

"Life is full of disappointments," said Christy. "Go look around."

Alan stood there, trying to think of something cool to say, but somehow Christy left him tongue-tied. Christy pointed at Tim.

"His birthday's next week," she explained. "My mom told me to take him shopping." As Tim disappeared among the shelves of toys, Christy smiled at Alan and began to look around the store.

"You're Christy, right?" Alan said, as if he didn't know the name of the girl of his dreams.

"Right," replied Christy.

"I'm Alan Abernathy. We moved into the house behind yours."

Christy didn't even look up. "I've seen you around."

Alan blinked. "You have?" he said.

"Yeah—how come I never see you around after school?"

Alan explained that his afternoons were generally spent working at The Inner Child.

Christy took a good look at the musty little store. Finally she spoke. "My suggestion? Torch the place."

From the back of the shop came a loud thump. "Victory will be ours!" a voice said. Alan grinned. Little Tim must have found the Small Soldiers.

Tim ran to the front of the store. "I know what I want! I want the soldiers! They were walking and fighting—they're so cool!"

He dragged Christy to the back of the store. Alan followed.

"How much are these?" Christy asked Alan. When he told her the price, her eyes widened in shock.

"There's no way Mom and Dad are going to buy you one of these," she said.

"Yes, they will," said Tim. "They buy you your Gwendy dolls."

"As if," said Christy sarcastically and then turned to Alan. "I haven't played with dolls since I was in preschool."

"What about the Massage Therapist Gwendy you got for your birthday?" persisted Tim. "And the one with the hidden tattoo?"

Christy realized her younger brother was determined to embarrass her into doing what he wanted, and decided it was a battle she couldn't win. "Save me one of the buff guys," she said to Alan.

"And a monster," said Tim.

"I don't think so," said Christy. As Tim began to protest, Alan headed the argument off at the pass.

"Look, I'll hold it for you till tomorrow," he said.

"Well, 'bye," said Christy. "Say hi once in a while."

"You got it," said Alan, cocking his index finger at her like a gun. He immediately regretted the lame move. Christy's amused grin didn't help matters any.

The door closed behind them.

"Congratulations," Alan said to Chip Hazard. "You're almost sold." Then he picked up Archer, with his pug-ugly face and scaly legs. "You, I'm not so sure about," he said. He left the two on a nearby table.

That's when he noticed his dad's plane tickets. He'd left them behind. If Alan rushed, he might just get them to his dad in time for him to catch the plane. Alan grabbed his backpack. Although he was in a rush, he made sure to carefully lock up the store for the night. He was going to do everything right for a change.

But it wasn't burglars Alan should have been worrying about. The danger to his dad's store was already inside.

# CHAPTER 4

In the backyard of a suburban house, the world's most annoying neighbor revved the engine of the world's most oversized lawn tractor. In Phil Fimple's eyes, big was beautiful—and noisy was even better.

Perhaps the only thing that made more noise than the lawn tractor was Phil's chainsaw. And Phil had the perfect excuse to use it.

As the saw roared to life, Stuart Abernathy stuck his head out of the window.

"Hey, knock that off!" he yelled.

"Stu," said Phil casually. "Satellite dish guy says this tree's gotta go. You don't mind, do you?"

Stuart struggled to maintain his composure. For a long moment nothing happened. Then Stuart stormed outside, walked up to the fence between the two properties, and said, between clenched teeth, "Yes, I mind."

Phil looked at him, his brain whirring, and finally said, "I'll check on the zoning laws. But I think they'll prove I'm in the right here."

Just as Stuart was about to go nuclear, Alan coasted up the driveway and handed him the airline tickets. Stuart blinked at them. "Thanks," he said gratefully. "Way to stay heads up."

"Sometimes I do something right," said Alan. As Stuart hopped into his car and drove away, Alan's mother, Irene, began running through a list of things Alan might have forgotten to do at the store.

"So the door was locked when you left?"

"Uh-huh."

"Did you empty the register?"

"Both quarters and all six pennies," said Alan. "And I shut off the lights, okay?"

"I'm just asking—"

"And I'm telling you—I did everything. You know, it's possible I might be able to make it through an entire day without screwing up."

Irene looked at him uncertainly. She wanted to believe she could rely on him, but . . . Alan knew that expression. It made him *so* mad. He threw open the front door and went inside.

Up in his room he glanced briefly at the posters of supermodels and superheroes on the walls, switched on his computer, reached into his saddlebag—and almost jumped out of his skin.

Something was moving inside.

"What the—" The bag moved again. Alan peered into it. The Gorgonite monster called "Arch-Fiend" looked back at him.

"How did you get in there?" Alan exclaimed.

He reached inside the bag and pulled the monster out.

"Greetings. I am Archer, emissary of the Gorgonites."

Alan held him up. "Beware! There will be no mercy," Archer said.

"Is that so?" said Alan.

"I am Archer, emissary of the Gorgonites," said Archer. "What is your name?"

"I'm Alan, now shut up," said Alan. "I've got homework." He turned back to the computer.

"Greetings, Alan-Now-Shut-Up," said Archer.

Alan spun around. "What did you just say?" he asked.

The toy said nothing.

"You just said my name," Alan insisted.

Still nothing.

Alan shook his head and returned to his homework.

Meanwhile, in the dark and silent toy store, something strange was going on. The silence was replaced by a faint but steady *Whap! Whap! Whap!* from a shelf at the back of the store. Major Chip Hazard, the buckle of his belt glowing brightly, was punching away at the plastic window of his display box, trying to get out.

Across the video screen through which he viewed the world scrolled masses of code and data. "PRIMARY COMMANDO-MENT: Destroy all Gorgonites."

Moments later he was standing on the shelf, looking up at the boxes of the other Commandos.

"Commandos! Fall in!" he shouted. Inside each box the soldiers' buckle lights came on—and they, too, began to punch their way out of their packages.

Soon they were all standing at attention before their commander.

"Sound off, soldiers!" yelled Chip.

"Link Static, communications. Awaiting dispatch of orders, sir!" said the first.

"Brick Bazooka, artillery! Ready to go full-bore, sir!" said a trooper with arms like tree trunks.

"Kip Killigan, covert insurgent, sharp as a razor,

sir!" announced a weasel-faced mercenary with a heart tattoo on his biceps.

"Butch Meathook, sniper," said a bearded soldier. "Prepared to go the distance, sir!"

"Whoo-wee! Nick Nitro, demolitions," yelled a maniacal figure with a punk haircut. "Armed and ready, sir!"

Chip looked at them with satisfaction. "Our mission: Destroy the Gorgonite enemy," he said. "Defeat him."

The Commandos replied, as one, with a tremendous yell. "Yes, sir!"

Chip held his rifle above his head, then snapped it in half. "This ordnance is insufficient," he said. "We must requisition weapons. Commandos, fall out!"

Safe at home in bed, Alan slept like a baby. Archer, who hadn't moved since he'd learned Alan's name was Alan-Now-Shut-Up, slowly began to come to life. A hand moved, then a foot. He took a step— and turned to look down at the sleeping Alan.

Satisfied that he wouldn't be observed, Archer walked over to the computer and tilted the screen down so he could see it easily. Using both hands, he pressed the "on" button.

Microsoft Encarta came scrolling down the screen, and Archer's eyes widened. Every now and then he'd use the mouse button to stop and examine something more carefully—then on he'd go, plunging further and further, with greater and greater delight, into the world of knowledge.

Then, his face brightly lit by the glow of the screen, he reached out to touch it.

"Home," said Archer softly to himself.

"What the heck are you?" said a voice behind him, and Archer almost jumped out of his plastic skin. Alan was awake. "You're not like any toy I've ever seen. Come on, speak up."

"Greetings, Alan-Now-Shut-Up," said Archer. "I am Archer, emissary of the Gorgonites."

"Uh-huh," said Alan. "I think you're smarter than you let on."

Archer said nothing.

"You're smart enough to get my name right, I bet. It's just plain 'Alan.' That's all. Got it?"

There was a pause. Then Archer said, "Greetings, Alan,"

"I knew it!" said Alan. "Walk to the end of the desk."

Archer hesitated.

"Don't play dumb," said Alan. "You know what I'm saying."

Archer thought for a moment, walked to the end of the desk, turned, and came back.

"Alan. Friend of Archer," he said. "Defender of all

Gorgonites. Keeper of Encarta. You must help us."

Alan looked at him, puzzled.

"The Gorgonites must be free," said Archer.

Alan picked him up and looked for the "off" switch. There wasn't one.

"There will be no mercy," said Archer.

"Right. Say something else," said Alan.

"There will be no mercy!" Archer repeated.

"Maybe you're not as smart as I thought," said Alan. He picked up Archer and shoved him in his desk drawer.

"Beware! There will be no mercy," came a muffled voice.

*Tomorrow*, Alan thought, *he's going back to the store*.

Back at that very store, Major Chip Hazard and his men had looted Stuart's workbench and replaced all their plastic weapons with fearsome-looking devices made from Stuart's tools. With a jigsaw puzzle of the American flag behind him, Chip addressed them once more.

"Soldiers," he began. "No poor sap ever won a war by dying for his country, he won it by being all that he can be, damn the torpedoes, or give me death! Eternal vigilance is the price of duty, and to the victor go the spoils!" His voice began to rise. "So remember—you are the best of the best of the few and the proud. So ask not what your country can do for you, only regret that you have one life to give!"

The Commandos cheered.

"The war against the Gorgonites will be won!" Chip announced. "Commando Elite—let the first shot be fired. Search out the Gorgonites—and frag them all!" As he uttered these words, Brick Bazooka and Nick Nitro lit a match and held it to the end of the flamethrower Chip had made from a butane lighter.

A jet of flame shot out.

The war had begun.

## CHAPTER 5

The next morning Alan arrived at the toy store, unlocked the door, stepped inside, and fumbled for the lights.

And stopped dead, looking around him in horror.

The shop looked like a war zone. Almost everything in it had been hurled off the shelves. Piles of broken toys lay in the aisles. His father's workbench was almost empty. As Alan stared, hardly able to believe his eyes, Archer slipped out of his backpack and hurried through the wreckage, searching for the other Gorgonites. Almost immediately he came upon the twisted, broken torso of Troglokhan, his head lying at least a yard away from his body, his eyes staring into nothingness. "Beware! There will be no mercy," Archer said.

"I am in so much trouble," said Alan. He stared at the broken Commando boxes on the floor. "Who did this?" he said to Archer.

Archer silently pointed to the Commando Elite display.

"No way," said Alan.

"The Commando Elite will destroy the Gorgonites," said Archer.

"No way," said Alan, "am I taking the blame for this!"

He picked up one of the boxes and read the words: "PROBLEMS? CALL OUR TOY HOTLINE: 1-800-GLOBOTK." He scooped up the pieces of Troglokhan and dialed the number while Archer climbed sadly into the wreckage of one of Stuart's wooden ships. After a moment, a computer voice answered.

"Welcome to Globotech! For GlobotecTronics, press one and the pound sign now. For PetroChemTech, press two and the pound sign now. For Gourmand Foods, press three and the pound sign now. For Heartland Play Systems, press four and the pound—"

Alan pressed four and waited for a human voice. He was finally put through to the Toy Division—where the same voice announced that all the operators were busy serving other customers.

That's when the ad started.

"A new age has dawned—for action! The Commando Elite—everything else is just a toy!"

Alan slammed down the phone in frustration.

There was a knock at the door. "Sorry, we're closed—" Alan started to say, when he realized it was Christy.

"I'll be real quick. I just came to get those toys," she said. "The Major Chip thing and one of the monsters. Tim actually got my folks to cave."

"Sorry," said Alan. "I can't sell you the toys."

"But—you're the only store that has them," Christy said.

"The toys are gone, all right?" said Alan, thinking on his feet. "They've been stolen."

Christy looked around and for the first time saw the devastation. "Are you pulling some sort of insurance scam?" she said.

"Do I look stupid?" Alan asked. "The policy wouldn't pay off to *me*."

Christy blushed. "Well, it's just—I've heard about, you know, your reputation. . . ."

"Oh, man!" Alan exploded. "I swear, you do one thing wrong, and that's it, you're branded for life!"

"Wait—you mean it's true?" Christy cried. "But I heard your folks had to move here because you got kicked out of *ten* different schools."

"No," said Alan. He paused for a beat. "It was two."

Christy grinned. She looked around the wrecked store. "Do you need some help?"

Alan heaved a huge sigh of relief.

A couple of hours later most of the debris was gone, the remains of a fast-food meal were scattered on the counter, and Christy was gluing a wooden ship back together. Alan was telling her all about his checkered past. It involved bad cafeteria food, security locks, and some neat tricks with contact cement. Christy looked appropriately impressed.

"You know all that stuff they say about how your permanent record's going to follow you forever?" He paused. "It's true."

Christy looked serious. "You know," she began, "I kind of know how you feel. Everyone expects *me* to be cheerful and nice all the time. And I get so sick of it. It's like I'm genetically doomed to life as Cheerleader Gwendy."

Alan studied her for a moment. "I don't know," he said. "You seem pretty negative to me."

Christy smiled. "Really?" she said. "Thanks!"

Alan looked at the finished boat in her hands. "Hey, that looks great!" he said.

For a minute they looked at each other, each knowing they had found a friend. Then the door opened and Stuart walked in. "Hey, Alan, how's it going?" he said, trying to be casual. "I was just on my way home from the airport, thought I'd stop by."

"And check up on me," said Alan.

"No! Of course not!" said Stuart. But he proceeded to look around the store. His tour of inspection lasted about one minute before he knew something was wrong.

"What happened here?" he demanded.

"Nothing—nothing happened," said Alan. What had they missed? They *hadn't* missed anything, he was sure. But Christy noticed three things they'd forgotten: Archer, his box, and the broken body of Troglokhan.

"Then how do you explain *this*?" Stuart asked, pointing to his ship. He touched the mast and it cracked in two. He was furious.

"Uh—I should go," said Christy. Then, pretending to remember something, she went over to the counter, scooped up Archer, the box, and Troglokhan, and slipped away before Stuart could see them.

"You should go on home, too," Stuart said. "I'll close up."

"I can do it," said Alan.

"No, obviously, you can't," Stuart snapped. "Go home."

Christy was waiting for him as he came out of the shop. "Sorry about that," Alan said sheepishly.

"I've got parents, too," said Christy. "If that's all he sees, you got off lucky." She handed him Archer, Troglokhan, and the box. "Here are your toys," she said. Alan took them, hot with embarrassment—just as Brad, Christy's upperclassman boyfriend and school jock, pulled up on his motorcycle. He looked at Alan. "I know you," he said slowly. "You're the guy who set his old school on fire, right?"

Alan stared him down. "Yep," he said, straight-faced. "Just to watch it burn."

Brad stared at Alan as if he were a mutant. "Whatever," he said. Christy hopped on the motorcycle and put on her helmet. The two blasted away. Brad had a cool motorcycle *and* Christy. And all Alan had was . . . He looked down at the toys in his hands. Angrily, he threw the remains of Troglokhan in the dumpster.

*What a mess*, thought Alan. He'd made himself look like a complete idiot in front of the two people he really wanted to impress, Christy and his dad. Now his dad would never trust him. And Christy—Christy must think he was a serious loser.

As he watched the motorcycle disappear around the corner he couldn't remember feeling this bad— ever.

# CHAPTER 6

Alan stuffed Archer and the box into his saddlebag. *I don't know why I'm doing this*, he thought. *I'm too old for toys*. But despite this, he bungee-corded the saddlebag to the bike rack and set off for home.

He was completely unaware that he was being watched by a small plastic figure perched on a telephone pole.

Link Static pressed the communicator control on his belt buckle. "Link Static to Command Post," he barked. "Target spotted. Approaching your position. Over."

A block away, hidden behind a bush, the rest of

the Commandos observed Alan cycling toward them. Chip rested a pair of binoculars on Butch Meathook's back. "Brick Bazooka, front and center," he rapped out. "Prepare for assault, Sergeant."

As Alan cycled toward them, lost in dark thoughts, Brick Bazooka held tight to the rubber band. The rest of the Commando Elite hauled it back as far as they could. "Steady, soldiers," said Chip. "Wait till you see the whites of their eyes." The bike got closer. "Now!" he yelled.

The Commandos released the rubber band, and Brick Bazooka shot out of the bush, firing a grappling hook toward the bike as he flew through the air. He hit the ground, the rope went taut, and he bounced along behind the bike, hauling himself hand over hand along the rope toward it.

Suddenly there was a tremendous barking noise. A huge dog came bounding along the sidewalk, teeth snapping. "Get out of here!" yelled Alan. On the ground, Brick drew up his legs to keep them out of range of the dog's snapping teeth—as Alan sped up and, without knowing it, saved him.

At last, as Brick hauled himself up to the bike itself, Alan made a right turn that sent him tumbling down onto the chain. Desperate not to be caught in it, Brick ran along the chain like a hamster on a wheel until Alan made a left turn, threw him into the spokes, and sent him crashing to the roadway—in two pieces. Alan cycled on, completely unaware of Brick's kamikaze mission.

Heroically, Brick hauled himself toward his lower half and hit his communications button.

"Brick Bazooka reporting, sir. Target escaped. Located enemy stronghold. Sir . . . I'm pretty messed up, sir."

"Link Static, lock in on his position," said Chip. Then, to Brick: "Hold on, son—we're on our way."

At home in his room, quite oblivious to the danger that was approaching, Alan was still trying to get through to Globotech. This time he finally heard not a recorded message, but a human voice.

"What is the name of the toy and what is the nature of the problem?" asked the voice.

"The Gorgonites and the Commando Elite," said Alan. "They wrecked my dad's store and ran off!"

"I'm sorry, but Heartland Play Systems does not replace lost toys," said the voice.

"I didn't lose them!" said Alan. "The Commando Elite wrecked my dad's store and destroyed the Gorgonites!"

"I'm sorry," said the voice, "but Heartland Play Systems does not replace lost toys."

"Look, is there a machine I can talk to?" pleaded

Alan. "Put on a machine!" Alan left a message and slammed down the phone.

"Alan—" Archer began.

Alan flopped down on his bed. *"Don't* talk to me," he said to Archer. "Not a word." He put on his earphones, switched on the music, and turned up the volume.

# CHAPTER 7

Deep inside the vast complex of buildings that housed Heartland Play Systems, Larry Benson sat in his darkened office as Irwin Wayfair played him the recording of Alan's desperate phone message.

"Your stupid Commando Elite wrecked my dad's store, destroyed your stupid Gorgonites, and ran off," said Alan's voice on the tape. "Lawsuit! Got that?"

"This is not a problem," said Larry dismissively. "What's the shelf date on this line? Monday, right? So how did this kid get them?" He paused for effect. "Industrial espionage. I have two words for you—

counter suit. One word. No, two words."

"Larry, what if he's telling the truth?" said Irwin. "We can't put toys on the market that may be dangerous!"

"And disappoint all those little kids who have their hearts set on owning the Commando Elite?" argued Larry. And you might almost have believed he cared about them.

Irwin sat down at his computer and pulled up the spec sheet on the Small Soldiers. Everything was fine until he got to one line—the computer chips.

"They were designed for the Department of Defense," said Irwin.

"They cost four thousand dollars," said Larry.

"We put munitions chips in toys," groaned Irwin.

"The guy said they were surplus!" said Larry. But now even he was worried.

Irwin snatched up his laptop and walked to the door. "We've got to find out what those chips do. And we've got to do it before Monday."

Larry nodded. "And we really have to rethink the sell-through price."

Meanwhile, as Alan lay in bed reading and listening to his headphones, Archer heard a muffled voice in the distance.

"Beware!" said the voice. "There will be no

mercy." Archer looked at Alan, but he hadn't heard a thing.

The little monster climbed quietly off the desk, slipped out the open door—and into the hallway.

"Beware! There will be no mercy!" said the muffled voice, louder now. Archer crept cautiously through the darkness. Who could it be? A surviving Gorgonite, come searching for his help?

At last he found it. The sound was coming from inside the hall cabinet. Archer pulled open the door and peered into the shadows. "Beware—there will be no mercy," said Major Chip Hazard—as Butch Meathook and Nick Nitro pounced on Archer and dragged him into the darkness.

When Archer came to, he was on the counter next to the kitchen sink. "Last chance, Gorgonite scum," said Chip Hazard.

"I am Archer, emissary of the Gorgonites," said Archer.

"We have ways of making you talk!" hissed Chip. "Where are the rest of the Gorgonite scum?"

A sudden ray of hope burst in Archer's heart—the other Gorgonites must be alive! He said nothing.

Chip's eyes flashed furiously. "Into the pit," he said. The Commandos dangled Archer over the whirling blades of the garbage disposal. Archer closed his eyes. His last moment had come, but there was no way was he going to betray his friends.

And then the kitchen light clicked on.

"Hey!" yelled Alan.

"Troopers, pull back!" snapped Chip. "Retrograde movement!" The Commando Elite scattered like cockroaches, slipping out through the cat door—and letting go of Archer.

As Archer dropped toward the whirling blades of the disposal, Alan dove forward and caught him. He reached for the disposal switch. Nick Nitro, who'd been left behind, jammed a saw blade into his arm.

"Surrender, Gorgonite ally!" Nick Nitro snarled.

"Owww!" yelled Alan—but he didn't let the pain stop him. He grabbed Nick's saw, cut Archer free, and thrust the Commando into the garbage disposal. Seconds later the blades separated Nick's legs from his body—and jammed the mechanism so it ground to a halt.

Alan's parents burst into the room. "What is going on in here?" yelled Stuart.

"Alan, your arm!" Irene cried.

"How did you cut yourself?" Stuart asked.

Alan didn't know what to say, where to begin. He took a deep breath and told his parents—the truth. "When you were gone, I got this shipment of soldier toys from Joe and I figured I could sell them while you were away and finally make some money for the store for once and I know it was wrong and I'm really sorry and there, I've said it."

Stuart and Irene looked at each other. "Well," Stuart began, "okay, that was very . . ." He searched for the right word. ". . . honest of you to tell the truth. So, what, you pawned my woodworking tools to pay Joe?"

Alan shook his head. "No, I'm pretty sure the toys took them."

Stuart lost it. "Are you *trying* to upset me?" he yelled.

"Archer, say something!" Alan pleaded. "Would you talk?" He began to shake him. But Archer's little plastic face remained rigid, his mouth shut like a trap.

"Alan, please," said Irene, "I have to ask you this—are you on drugs?"

"No!" Alan yelled. "The soldiers . . ."

Stuart interrupted him. "Alan—I'm at a loss." He sighed. "I'm really at a loss."

Irene shook her head despairingly. "Honey, go take care of that cut," she said. "Then go to bed."

Alan slowly walked to the door. He turned back. "The disposal's broken," he said.

Stuart and Irene stared after their son. They didn't notice Nick Nitro crawl from behind the flour canister, scale the windowsill, and disappear into the night.

# CHAPTER
## 8

It was dark in Christy's garage. Only a thin sliver of moonlight illuminated it. Into this shaft of light stepped Major Chip Hazard.

"Commando Elite—fall in," he commanded. The Commandos gathered around him.

"We have met the enemy," said Chip, "and he is big. He is fast. He has allied himself with the Gorgonite scum. The rules of engagement have changed."

He nodded at Link Static, who switched on the light, revealing that they were in the mother of all garages. It was absolutely crammed with power tools, hand tools, nails, screws, and old machines, with yet more junk hanging from the rafters and stuffed into corners. The Commandos gazed at it in awe. The possibilities were endless.

Nick Nitro—or what was left of him—tumbled in through the window.

"Medic!" he said. Chip hurried over. He quickly realized that there was nothing a medic could do— even if they had one.

"I'm messed up pretty bad, sir," Nick said weakly.

"Rest easy," said Chip. "You've done your job."

"Did we win?" asked Nick.

"We will," said Chip Hazard.

Nick seemed to smile—and then the light on his belt buckle went out. Chip stood up and addressed the troops, more determined than ever. "We must innovate, adapt, and overcome! Kip—secure the perimeter! Link—tap all communications! Butch— we are going to need to roll some armor! Brick—if it launches, lacerates, or detonates—I want it!" He paused. "Move it, you jarhead dogface leatherneck grunts! Hut! Hut! Hut!"

In the Abernathy bathroom, Alan angrily set Archer down on the counter. "Why didn't you say anything?" he demanded.

"'Don't talk to me. Not a word,'" said Archer, repeating Alan's instructions.

Alan ground his teeth as he put a bandage over

the cut on his arm. "Maybe I should just shred the bunch of you," he said. "My dad thinks I'm insane, Christy thinks I'm an idiot, and when Joe finds out those toys got destroyed he's gonna have my legs broken."

Archer looked up at him. "The Gorgonites are not destroyed," he said.

"What?" said Alan.

"Major Chip Hazard seeks the location of the Gorgonites. They are not destroyed."

Alan looked puzzled, then a look of realization crept over his face. "Because if the Commandos destroyed them, they wouldn't be *looking* for them."

Archer nodded.

"All right. So then, where are they?" Alan asked.

Archer looked up at him. "My Gorgonite brothers are doing what Gorgonites do best," he said proudly. "They are *hiding*."

# CHAPTER
## 9

In the Sunday morning silence of Winslow Corners, a boy was searching the shelves of an empty toy store. It was Alan, looking for the Gorgonites. He peered under counters, behind boxes, on top of cupboards. He emerged from the storeroom, empty-handed. "I can't find them." He shook his head. "Monsters shouldn't hide, anyway. You should be out shredding Commandos."

"We would lose," replied Archer sadly.

"You don't know that," said Alan.

"It is what we are programmed to do," replied Archer.

"Hide and lose," said Alan in disbelief. "Those are

great options." He thought for a moment, then pulled the Gorgonite box out of his backpack. "What about this? It says here you guys are supposed to be searching for your home."

"The Land of Gorgon." Archer nodded.

"Maybe they went to find it," suggested Alan.

"They would not go without me," Archer said.

Exasperated, Alan let out a deep breath. "All right. If I were a Gorgonite, where would I be? Okay, I'm hiding, I'm a loser, I've got zero self-esteem." That's when it hit him. He ran out to the alley and threw the dumpster lid open.

"Hey! You in there? It's safe!" he called. No reply. Dejected, he turned around. Another brilliant idea that hadn't worked out.

"Ocula!" cried Archer.

Alan spun around and came face to face with a giant eyeball.

In the dumpster, bags shifted, trash seethed and wriggled—and the rest of the Gorgonites began to emerge. As each one came out, Archer greeted them happily.

"Punch-It!" he said, as a creature that looked like a cross between a rhinoceros and a Triceratops appeared. A mouthful of teeth on top of two frog legs surged out of the trash. "Scratch-It!" said Archer. A devilish figure with teeth like a shark, one eye larger than the other, a necklace of teeth around its neck, and a body wrapped with chains emerged. "Insaniac!" said Archer. A caveman with massive feet used his club to haul himself into the light. "Slamfist," Archer announced. There was a pause. Then the creature formerly known as Troglokhan emerged. Patched together from broken bits of his own parts, broken pieces of other toys, and whatever else the Gorgonites had been able to find in the dumpster, he looked like something that Dr. Frankenstein would have rejected as being too weird.

"Troglokhan?" said Archer in disbelief.

"We fixed him," said Punch-It.

"Tried to fix him," said Slamfist.

"Some assembly required," Troglokhan rasped— and coming from him, it sounded deeply sarcastic.

Troglokhan hit a button on his chest and revealed that one of the parts used to repair him had come from an old radio. A song came out of the tinny speaker: "They did the mash, they did the monster mash."

"Freaky," said Alan. "Like Frankenstein."

"Freakenstein," said Archer, agreeing.

Alan stared at the group.

"At least you're all here," he said with a sigh. "Maybe Joe won't break my legs after all." He paused. "This is an improvement—I guess."

He rummaged through the dumpster one last time and found a large cardboard box. "Okay, everybody in!" he said.

# CHAPTER
## 10

Larry and Irwin, clad in big white suits like astronauts about to take a walk on the moon, pushed open the airlock door. They stepped into a "clean room" in the Globotech Defense Department. A "clean room" is a room in which not a single speck of dust is allowed to enter, in order to protect the delicate devices being made there. The air is cleaned and purified twenty-four hours a day—and every person going inside has to wear a special anti-static suit.

A technician was busy examining microchips under a microscope and didn't notice them.

"Hey! Hello!" said Larry.

The tech looked up. "You aren't supposed to be here," he said.

"It's me. Larry. You supplied my division with some microchips."

The technician nodded. "Ah yes—the X-1000. Worked out better than you dreamed didn't they? You're welcome."

"Yeah, thanks," said Larry. "But uh—there may be a problem."

The tech gave him a dead-eyed stare, then turned away. "Then it's with your software," he retorted.

Irwin gasped. *His* software? "Oh, I don't think so," he said huffily.

"Oh you don't?" sneered the technician. "The X-1000 is a masterpiece. Imagine a microprocessor sophisticated enough to control the guidance systems of ballistic missiles." He paused for effect. "Now imagine it can learn."

"You're talking about—*artificial intelligence*?" Irwin said with a gasp.

"No, *actual* intelligence," said the tech. "It's no wonder the Philistines in the Pentagon couldn't appreciate it. One tiny flaw and they scrap the whole project."

This gave Irwin a small ray of hope. "Aha! So there *is* a flaw in the hardware."

The tech looked at Irwin like he was a techno-idiot. "They're vulnerable to electromagnetic pulse. You know, the kind of EMP caused by the detonation of a nuclear device?" He sneered. "I doubt even the toy industry has become quite that competitive."

Outside the clean room, Larry and Irwin removed their suits. Irwin sat down dejectedly on a bench. "I'm going to call Mr. Mars. We have to recall the toys."

Larry stopped him. He was not putting his career on the line on the say-so of one squeaky-voiced kid from Bumpkinville, USA. They'd recall the shipment for the kid's area code. And that was all.

Irwin nodded grudgingly. "But what about the toys he has?" he asked.

Larry gave in. "I've always wanted to see Bumpkinville," he said with a sigh.

# CHAPTER
## 11

Alan and Archer surveyed the chaotic scene in Alan's bedroom. The entire place was crawling with Gorgonites. Alan's cat, Zorro, was perched out of harm's way on a shelf near the ceiling, looking down in alarm. Freakenstein clicked through the Encarta art gallery on Alan's computer, looking lovingly at one stunning painting after another and sighing heavily at all that beauty.

Ocula and Slamfist were watching TV, fascinated by a wrestling match. Ocula winced and hid behind his friend as a particularly painful-looking throw took down one of the wrestlers—but Slamfist banged his boulder hand in delight. This was just the kind of stuff he liked.

Punch-It sat on one end of the bed, apparently meditating. Scratch-It, on the other end, was busy finding out just how high he could bounce. On the desk, Insaniac was studying geography with the aid of a globe. Well, not exactly studying—his method was to spin the globe as fast as he could, jump on top of it, get flung off, and land in a corner laughing hysterically before doing the whole thing over again.

"What am I going to do with you guys?" said Alan.

As the wrestlers on TV performed a leap-off-the-turnbuckle-body-slam, Ocula shut his eye in horror and Slamfist banged his hand so excitedly he accidentally hit the remote control and switched channels.

To a station showing a movie. A woman had just taken off her clothes and was about to get into the shower. Slamfist stared. Ocula's eye grew wider than ever.

"Hey!" said Alan, coming over. "Your box said appropriate for age five!"

"Age five—and *up*," said Slamfist.

"Too bad," said Alan, and switched channels to an old black-and-white horror flick.

"Awww," said Slamfist disgustedly. But Ocula was

As usual, Larry was ready, willing, and able to pass the blame on to Irwin.

Mars squeezed Flatchoo's stomach. It let out a deep, satisfied belch, and Mars laughed in delight.

"How much are these?" Christy asked Alan. When he told her the price, her eyes widened in shock.

"Greetings. I am Archer, emissary of the Gorgonites."

Alan cycled on, completely unaware of Brick's kamikaze mission.

The Commandos dangled Archer over the whirling blades of the garbage disposal.

Chip nodded at Link Static, who switched on the light, revealing that they were in the mother of all garages.

Five...four...three...two... one...blast off!

Chip Hazard leaned over. "Are you scared?" he asked Christy. "We're all scared. You'd have to be crazy not to be scared."

Christy gasped in horror as the doll turned its face to the light. It had melted into the face of a zombie!

"I'm Irwin, I designed you!" said Irwin excitedly. "And all of the Gorgonites. You're all here!"

Another tank started firing flaming tennis balls through the broken window.

Chip's helicopter zoomed in from the direction of the house, firing as it came.

"We did what we do best," Archer said. "We hid."

delighted. The movie was called *The Crawling Eye*. He scurried over to the screen to get as close as he could.

"Not so close," said Alan. "You'll ruin your, uh, eye." He pushed Ocula back. *I'm beginning to sound just like my mom*, Alan thought.

As if on cue, his mother called from downstairs. "Alan!"

"Gorgonites, scatter and hide," said Archer.

A split second later there wasn't a Gorgonite to be seen.

"Geez," said Alan. "They *are* good."

Irene came into the room. "You had a call," she said. "From Christy. That's that darling girl next door, isn't it? Is that what this is all about?" she said hopefully. "A girl?"

"Mom!" said Alan, embarrassed.

"Call her back," said Irene, handing him a piece of paper and closing the door.

Alan sat down on his bed and looked at the number. The Gorgonites re-emerged and gathered around.

"What is Christy?" asked Punch-It.

"Not what, *who*," said Alan. "She's this girl. I wonder why she called."

"You should learn why," advised Archer.

"Yeah, yeah, learn," shouted Slamfist.

"I'm a little nervous to call her," Alan admitted.

"Nervous?" said Archer.

"Scared," replied Alan.

Freakenstein knew all about that. "If something scares you, you should hide," he remarked wisely.

"Beware!" said Punch-It. "Christy is the mortal enemy of Alan, defender of Gorgonites."

"She'll destroy you," said Archer, getting caught up in the excitement. This was the kind of stuff the Gorgonites had been programmed to know about.

"She'll hunt you down," said Slamfist.

"To the ends of the earth," added Freakenstein.

"No!" said Alan. "I really like her. I mean, she's—" he hesitated. "She's great."

"You aren't scared of her?" asked Archer.

"No, not like that," said Alan.

"Then there is no reason to hide," said Archer.

Alan looked at him—and finally nodded. "Good point." He took a deep breath, picked up the phone, and dialed the number. A moment later Christy answered.

"Hello?"

"Hi, Christy, it's Alan," said Alan. "My mom said you called."

"Yeah," said Christy. "So, did we get away with it?"

"What?" asked Alan, confused.

"You know, the store. Did your dad suspect anything?"

"Oh, no," Alan lied. "He doesn't suspect a thing."

"Great. I'm glad you didn't get in trouble, Alan," Christy said.

"Right," said Alan.

There was a very awkward silence.

"Well, okay," said Christy. The conversation seemed to be going nowhere. Any minute now Alan would have no choice but to hang up. Then he saw the Gorgonites staring at him, looking disappointed. "Christy!" he said.

"Yeah?" said Christy.

"I was wondering if . . . uh . . . if maybe you'd like to go to a movie or something sometime?"

There—he'd said it. He couldn't believe it—he'd said it. There was a pause at the other end of the line.

"Uh . . . I'm dating Brad," Christy finally said.

"Oh, right," said Alan.

"Alan, you're . . ." she paused again. "Too young for me."

"We're the same age," Alan argued.

"I know . . . I only date older guys. It's nothing personal."

"Oh, okay, right," said Alan.

"Besides," said Christy, a flirtatious note creeping

into her voice. "My mom thinks you're a bad influence."

"Really?" said Alan.

"Like you could really get me in trouble."

"Oh," said Alan, not quite getting it. "So, I guess, never mind," he said. "I wouldn't want anything to happen to you because of me."

There was a long, painful silence. Then Christy said, "Okay. 'Bye, Alan."

"'Bye," said Alan, and hung up. He scowled at the Gorgonites. "That's what I get for taking advice from toys," he said.

Christy hung up the phone, too, feeling strangely dissatisfied with the conversation. She would have felt a lot more dissatisfied if she'd been able to follow the phone line through the wall, out to the breezeway, and along to the telephone junction box . . .

. . . where Link Static was busy tapping the lines. Satisfied, he clipped through a set of wires and slid down a length of cable all the way to Christy's garage. He snapped to attention in front of Chip.

"Enemy transmission intercepted, sir," said Link with a crisp salute. Chip looked up from the strange war machine he was welding together out of bits and pieces from all over the garage. Link replayed

Alan's voice, recorded from the phone lines: "I wouldn't want anything to happen to you because of me."

Chip processed this—and then slapped Link on the back. "Put yourself in for a commendation," he said. "Soldiers!"

All over the garage the Commandos snapped to attention from their work.

"The enemy has revealed a weakness," said Chip. "We must act quickly to take advantage." Expressions of steely determination came onto the faces of the tiny soldiers.

"Commando Elite," said Chip. "Move out! Now! Go!"

# CHAPTER

## 12

In Christy's house the world's most annoying neigh-bor pointed his remote control at his wide-screen TV with a proud flourish. "Live, via satellite!" Phil said triumphantly. "Two hundred and fifty seven channels. Dolby stereo where available—and that's right here!" He clicked a button on the remote. "Ta-da!"

The huge television blared to life with the bone-crunching noise of a football game. Marion Fimple, Phil's wife, came in with a tray loaded with drinks, popcorn, and pretzels.

"What a great picture," said Marion. Phil beamed with pride.

"It's *perfect*," she said.

Phil's expression changed. "It looks fuzzy," he said, peering closer.

"I've never seen a picture so clear," insisted Marion.

"Maybe if I tweak the brightness a little," said Phil, fiddling with the remote control.

Marion sighed. It was going to be a long night.

The front doorbell rang.

"I'll get it!" yelled Christy.

She raced downstairs and flung open the door. It was Brad.

"Hey," said Brad.

"Hey," said Christy.

"Let's go," said Brad.

"You drove your motorcycle, right?" asked Christy.

"Yeah," said Brad.

Christy nodded. "'Bye Mom, 'bye Dad," she said. "Don't wait up." And she went out the door.

The street echoed with the sound of an engine being revved as Brad accelerated away, forcing Christy, sitting behind him, to grab hold of his waist to avoid being thrown off.

"It's fuzzy, see? There's a ghost image," said Phil, still fiddling with the remote control.

"There's no ghost," said Marion, with a sigh.

"I see a ghost," insisted her husband. He was so busy concentrating on the giant screen that he didn't see an enormous shadow looming behind him. If he had, in fact, he would have been deceived, because the huge shadow didn't come from a huge figure but from tiny Chip Hazard and two of his Commandos, creeping into the room.

The soldiers focused on the two glasses sitting on the coffee table. Marion reached over, picked hers up, and took a long sip. Chip looked at his comrades, Butch and Kip, and jerked his thumb upstairs.

Seconds later they were going through the bathroom medicine cabinet, rummaging through hair spray, shampoo, and aspirin until they found what they were looking for—sleeping pills. Chip hauled out the bottle and tossed it down to Kip.

"Chemical warfare," he said.

They sneaked back downstairs. Kip loaded his launcher with a sleeping pill. Butch aimed it at the two glasses, and Chip gave the signal to fire.

The missile soared high into the air, passed over the two glasses, and landed somewhere in the kitchen. Neither of the humans noticed a thing. The Commandos looked at one another, shook off their first failure, reloaded the launcher, and tried again.

This time the missile dropped right into drink number one.

"You hear something?" asked Marion. The Commandos froze, but Phil shook his head.

"No. The sound is fine," he said. He gulped his drink and looked up at the screen again. "Huh," he said. "Now it's fuzzy *and* wavery."

Three more missiles rained down—two sleeping pills in each glass. As Chip watched the humans drink them down, he jerked his thumb again. Time to move out. Now when Marion looked at the screen, she realized Phil had been right.

"Look at that," she said. "It *is* fuzzy." And her head lolled back. Seconds later, she was asleep. As for Phil, he was already snoring.

Up on the roof, Brick Bazooka and Link Static were wrapped in fishing line, fishhooks secured to the rain gutter.

"Let's do it," said Link.

They threw themselves backward off the roof and rappeled down the wall toward Christy's open window with all the practiced skill of a SWAT team, then hurled themselves into the room.

They barrel-rolled onto the floor and came up fighting. "AAAAAAAAHHHHHH!" they yelled—as Chip and the rest of the Commandos raced in through the door, yelling "AAAAAAAAHHHHHH!" in their turn. Only to realize the room was empty— they were pointing their guns at one another. Their yells died in their throats, and they looked around sheepishly.

Chip took charge. "Our target has taken evasive action," he said. "Fan out. Recon the area."

The light switched on. The Commandos froze.

"Hey—cool," said a voice. It was Tim. He stared down at the Commandos as if it were Christmas morning. "Oh, man," he said. "I can't believe they got me the whole set!" He flopped down on the floor right next to Chip.

"Hold your fire, men," said Chip.

"Cool," said Tim. "You can talk." He looked at Chip. "You must be the leader." Sitting down cross-legged, he began to play. "Except one day you get shot—bam!" He knocked Chip over. "And then," he said, picking up Kip, "Kip Killigan gets promoted, and now *he's* the leader."

Tim walked Kip around, making him salute. As he lay on his back, a determined expression came onto Chip's face. This was humiliating. "Commandos—attack!" said Chip.

As the Commandos swarmed toward him, Tim laughed with delight and started knocking them down, picking them up, and slamming them against one another.

Down below, in the living room, Phil Fimple came blearily half awake, shouting, "Whazzat—a war zone up there?" He immediately fell back asleep.

Had he been able to make it up to Christy's room, he would have come across a scene like the end of a battle—Commandos sprawled everywhere, many of them pretty beat-up. Those that weren't had taken cover. Tim was the victor. But, of course, for him this was only half the game. "Okay, now I'm a prisoner of war," he announced as he surveyed the defeated Commandos. "Go ahead, capture me."

He knelt down with his hands behind his back. Chip looked out from under Christy's bed, incredulous—and immediately took advantage of the changed situation. He jerked his head toward Kip and Brick. They rushed forward and wrapped fishing line around and around Tim's wrists.

"Hey, that *hurts*," said Tim, trying to pull his hands free. The fishing line dug into his skin. "Hey, this isn't fun! Hey—"

But he didn't get to say much more, because Brick and Kip immediately jerked him backward and slapped duct tape over his mouth. "Mmmmfff!" he said as they proceeded to tie his legs together with yet more fishing line.

Only then did the Commandos look up and see two shelves full of Gwendy dolls. They stared at them, transfixed.

"Sir!" said Brick.

"R & R, sir?" asked Kip.

Chip looked up at the dolls—Hidden Tattoo Gwendy, Networking Gwendy, Urban Cowgirl Gwendy, Navy SEAL Gwendy. "Denied," he said. "Gentlemen, those are reinforcements. Maintain your discipline! Bring me Nick Nitro's body. Move!"

The Commandos dragged Nick's body bag over to Chip and unzipped it. Chip knelt down and cradled Nick's head in his arms. "Soldier," he said softly, "your memory will live on."

And then he yanked Nick's head off, broke it open—and pulled out the gleaming silicon microprocessor chip that had been Nick's brain.

# CHAPTER
## 13

Christy's room looked like a makeshift Dr.
Frankenstein's laboratory. Kip Killigan and Brick
Bazooka stood beneath a magnifying desk lamp,
wearing surgical masks made of adhesive bandages.
On the table lay Massage Therapist Gwendy, with a
handkerchief draped over her. Brick quickly shaved
her head with an electric razor.

Clumps of synthetic hair dropped in a pile around
the table as Chip looked down from above.
Narrowing his eyes, he switched on a cake mixer.

The blades of the cake mixer turned, winding up a
piece of string, which was attached to the engine of

a toy racing car. The engine was winched up to the operating table and lowered toward the patient. Kip leaned toward her with his welder. Sparks reflected off the sunglass lens he was using to protect his eyes.

Link removed a microchip from a gutted pocket calculator and slapped it into Kip's hand. Behind him lay a pile of remote controls, car alarms, portable phones—all the techno junk Phil Fimple had accumulated over the years, all with their microchips ready to be removed.

Her operation successfully completed, Massage Therapist Gwendy was lifted from the operating table and laid carefully down among a circle of post-op Gwendies. Wires snaked out of their heads to the transformer from a train set. Into this central point Chip Hazard now inserted the powerful silicon chip he'd taken from Nick Nitro's head. He threw the switch.

The entire circle of wired-up Gwendies twitched and jerked as electricity coursed through them and their new brains came to life. Then Chip turned off the power and looked to see what he had achieved.

Massage Therapist Gwendy sat up, the wires pulling out of her head. Jerkily, she got to her feet and snapped to attention.

"Massage Therapist Gwendy reporting for duty!"

she said. And gave a little wave. "Hi there," she added.

Chip decided that a wave was the best sort of salute he could expect from a Gwendy doll, and saluted her back.

Outside, Brad and Christy roared up to the house on the motorcycle.

"Mom, Dad, I'm home!" called Christy as she opened the front door. She saw Phil and Marion asleep on the couch. "They're asleep," she said.

Brad had followed her in. "You know what that means?" he said. Christy started to edge him toward the door.

"It means they could wake up any second," she answered.

Brad leered at her. "You are such a major hottie," he said.

"And you are such a major sweet-talker," said Christy, giving him a peck on the cheek and a gentle push out the door. "Good night." She closed the door behind him.

Sighing a little, she shrugged off her jacket and opened the closet door. On the floor, bound and gagged, was her little brother Tim.

"Mmmmmfff!" said Tim, desperately trying to get her attention. But the closet was dark and Christy was thinking about other things, so she simply tossed her jacket inside and shut the door.

"Mmmmfff!" said Tim, as the coat settled down over his head. Toy soldiers? He never wanted to see another toy soldier again!

Meanwhile Christy headed upstairs to her room and flipped the light switch. When nothing happened she walked through the dark room to the desk and switched on the desk lamp. The door slammed behind her.

Christy whirled around, but there was nothing there. Suddenly the lamp slid across the desk and crashed to the floor. As it did, Christy saw something disappear underneath her bed.

By the light of the fallen desk lamp Christy saw a bizarre sight—several of her precious Gwendy dolls lay in a circle, wired to a central transformer. Her mouth fell open as one of the dolls opened its eyes and sat up. "That is true cool!" the doll said.

"If I look nice, everyone will like me," said Talking Gwendy. Christy gasped in horror as the doll turned its face to the light. It had melted into the face of a zombie!

Christy screamed at the top of her lungs.

Brad was sitting astride his motorcycle outside the house trying to think of some lame excuse to knock on Christy's door when he heard the scream. His face lit up. He didn't need an excuse to come in—he was needed!

He leapt off the bike and raced toward the house. "Christy, I'm coming!" he yelled.

He ran up the darkened stairs, burst into Christy's room—and stopped dead. He couldn't believe what he was seeing. There was Christy, tied up with electrical cord like Gulliver in *Gulliver's Travels*, gagged with a pair of her own tennis socks!

And surrounding her was a set of the most evil-looking dolls he'd ever seen, all glaring at him.

"What the heck—" said Brad. But that was all he could manage before one of the evil Gwendies leapt up and fastened herself to his shirt front.

"Hi," said the Gwendy. "You're cute!"

Another doll leapt onto his head. "Will you take me to the prom?" she simpered.

And a third. "Do you want to see my tattoo?" she asked.

As more and more Gwendies threw themselves at Brad, hitting and kicking him, he completely freaked out. He spun around, slapping at them. "No way! No way!" he wailed. He stumbled to the bedroom door—to find Chip Hazard and the Commando Elite blocking his way.

Chip scowled. "An officer and a gentleman does not hit ladies!' he said. Butch Meathook stepped forward, brandishing a flamethrower. He pointed, aimed, and shot.

"Ow! Ow!" shouted Brad as his jeans began to burn. Suddenly he was half falling, half hopping down the stairs, finally making it through the front door and abandoning the jeans in the entryway. Seconds later he leapt onto his motorcycle and roared away down the street.

Upstairs, the Commandos came through the door of Christy's room pushing her dad's video camera on its wheeled tripod.

Chip Hazard leaned over. "Are you scared?" he asked Christy. "We're all scared. You'd have to be crazy not to be scared."

Christy wasn't crazy—she was petrified.

# CHAPTER
## 14

Meanwhile in Alan's room, Ocula stood at the window peering through a telescope. He began making alarmed-sounding noises. Alan scrambled up and crossed the room. "What?" he asked. "What do you see?"

At that moment something smashed through his window, shot across the room, and pinned Ocula to the wall. It was a barbecue fork, and it had a video-cassette taped to it. Around the videocassette was a piece of paper.

A single word was written on it: SURRENDER. Alan licked his lips nervously and pushed the videocas-sette into his VCR.

"Oh no," he whispered as the tape began to play. There, on-screen, was Christy, with a sheaf of papers in her hands. She read in a halting voice: "I am safe. I have not been harmed. I am making this statement of my own free will and under no duress." She looked right at the camera. "Yeah, right," she said— and then yelped as somebody off-camera poked her with something sharp.

"Ow—okay," she said, and continued reading. "The Commando Elite cannot be defeated. They will crush their enemies under their boots. They will . . ." She began to flip through the pages. "It goes on like that for a while." Another poke from off-camera. "I'm doing it, I'm doing it!" She resumed reading again. "I will be released, safe and unharmed, only if the following conditions are met. One: Surrender the Gorgonite scum! Two—" She flipped through the pages. "Uh . . . that's it." Then she looked at the camera again. "Alan—please—you have to—"

The image began to waver, and then the picture disappeared entirely. All Alan and the Gorgonites could see was snow.

For a long moment Alan stared at the screen without saying anything, his fists clenched in anger. He looked down at the Gorgonites. They were trembling with fear.

"If Major Chip Hazard wants a war, we'll give him a war!" he shouted.

Archer stepped forward. "No, Alan. We will give up," he said. "It is what we were born to do."

Alan looked at him and slowly shook his head. "Stop doing what you are expected to do just because that's how you're programmed." He stood up. "Are you going to let yourself get beat by a bunch of stupid toys?"

He strode toward the door, then paused when he realized whom he was talking to. "No offense," he said.

"None taken," said Punch-It. And meant it.

# CHAPTER 15

On the dark front step of the Fimple house sat a huge cardboard box. The word "Gorgonites" was scrawled across the side in black marker, and it was duct-taped shut and wrapped in thick twine. Pathetic cries came from inside the box. "We're afraid!" "Let us go!" "Alan, please don't do this!"

Meanwhile, a boy crept across the darkness of the Fimples' yard with something clutched to his chest.

Alan and Archer were going into battle.

In the Fimple living room, Phil and Marion still slept while Butch Meathook patrolled the area in a toaster tank. Chip watched as Brick Bazooka and Nick Nitro stood guard by the front door.

The doorbell rang. "Enemy contact," said Chip. "Advance with caution. Roll!"

●—●—●

Five . . . four . . . three . . . two . . . one . . . blast off!

Alan launched Archer, strapped to a toy rocket, into the air.

High above Christy's house, Archer released a parachute made from a white garbage bag. It blossomed out into the air. As he drifted down, Archer leaned to one side, spilling some air, gently angling toward the chimney.

He floated down the chimney and landed in the fireplace. Cutting his parachute free, he crept toward the breezeway door to let Alan in. He left a trail of sooty footprints on the carpet behind him.

Alan grabbed Archer and stuffed him into his knapsack. He crept stealthily up the stairs, reached the door of Christy's room, and cautiously opened it.

Christy made muffled noises through her gag—but Alan was in too much of a hurry to take any notice.

"It's okay!" he said, rushing over to her. He cut her ropes and took off the gag.

"Behind you!" shouted Christy the second she could speak—as the massed Zombie-Gwendy dolls began their attack, armed with sewing needles, razor-blade spears, and knives.

Alan whirled around. Startled and off-balance, he fell to the ground. A Zom-Gwendy raised a sharp needle above his throat. Christy sprang into action. She leapt off the bed and grabbed her baton. Swinging it wildly, she sent the Zom-Gwendies flying all over the room like so many ping-pong balls.

"You're all going to the Island of Misfit Toys!" she yelled. She swept the baton across the shelf with the rest of the Gwendies on it, sending them crashing to the floor.

"Christy?" said Alan. Before he knew what was happening, Christy grabbed him and gave him a huge kiss. Alan's eyes bulged in shock for a moment—and then he relaxed into it.

"You rescued me," said Christy softly when the kiss was done.

"Yes, I did," said Alan. Christy kissed him once more, then brought the baton smashing down on the desk top. "I just want one clean swing at the leader!" she said. "That's all! Come on!"

# CHAPTER

## 16

Out on the porch, the Commandos surrounded the cardboard box. The voices of the Gorgonites still echoed plaintively from inside. Brick Bazooka punched a hole through the side with a drill saw, and Kip dropped a chunk of explosive neatly inside. The Commandos grinned at one another—the Gorgonites were done for. Seconds later, the box blew up—to reveal the ruins of a tape recorder. There wasn't a Gorgonite in sight. The Commandos ground their little plastic teeth. They'd been fooled—by experts!

Alan and Christy slowly crept down the stairs—and were spotted by a toaster tank, which immediately began firing red-hot CDs at them. They dashed back into Christy's room and over to the window.

"We can get out across the patio cover!" said Christy.

"You've done this before?" said Alan.

"Once or twice," said Christy evasively as she swung her legs over the windowsill.

Seconds later they were on the ground, racing across the lawn. As they crossed the driveway, the garage door exploded.

The blast knocked them flat. As they struggled to get back up, the smoke cleared and they saw a huge hole in the garage door. Out roared the attack vehicles the Commando Elite had built out of all the equipment in Phil's garage. They were firing steak knives, corncob holders, and any other sharp implement they had been able to lay their hands on.

One of them shattered a car window, setting off an alarm. Several corncob holders slammed into Alan's thigh and he went down with a cry of pain, dropping the pack—with Archer inside—as he fell.

"Expect no mercy!" said Chip. And he wouldn't have given any, either, had Christy not jumped on her motor scooter, spun around, and knocked him and his tank right out of the way with her rear wheel.

"C'mon!" she said. Alan scrambled up onto the back.

"Archer!" said Alan urgently. "We gotta get Archer!"

Christy turned the scooter around. Alan scooped the trembling pack out of the vehicle's path and they took off.

But as they headed back toward Alan's house, a line of Commando Elite vehicles spread out across the road in front of them—and a hail of missiles shot out.

Christy did a U-turn and took off in the other direction.

Alan winced as he pried the corncob holders out of his leg.

"Alan, are you all right?" asked Archer, concerned.

"It's not bad," Alan replied. "I'm fine—" He glanced back and saw—nothing.

"Did we lose them?" asked Christy.

"I don't know!" said Alan. "Just keep going! We gotta find help!" He looked back again into the darkness. "Maybe we *did* lose them," he said.

Christy turned the scooter onto a wide bike path surrounded by tall trees. Suddenly one fell over, bursting into flames as it crashed to the ground. At the last minute Christy swerved around it.

"Interlock!" shouted Chip.

"Interlock!" repeated Link—and all three vehicles slid into one another until they formed one single vehicle with the power of all the individual vehicles combined. It began gaining on the scooter, Chip at the helm.

Archer looked back and saw the mega-vehicle. "Alan," he said.

When Alan turned around, his eyes nearly bugged out of his head. "Oh, man," he breathed. "They got bigger."

Just then the base of another tree exploded. But there was no time to get out of the way.

"Down!" screamed Christy. She ducked—and the tree hit Alan squarely in the head, knocking him right off the bike.

"Alan!" screamed Christy, screeching to a stop.

The mega-vehicle speeding toward him, Alan scrambled to his feet and raced for the scooter. He leapt onto the back. As Christy gunned away, a telephone pole fell right in front of them, blocking their path.

"Uh-oh," said Christy.

Ahead of them was a grassy picnic area with a path leading to the edge of a stream.

"I dare you," said Alan.

"Hang on," warned Christy—and hit the accelerator. At the edge of the stream, the scooter flew into the air. It landed hard, but safe, on the other side.

The mega-vehicle accelerated toward the bank of the stream.

Flew into the air just like the scooter . . .

. . . and crashed straight into the side of the ravine, hitting it with a noise like the end of the world. Pieces of the mega-vehicle and chunks of plastic Commando parts flew into the air and rained down like confetti. It was over. The Commando Elite were down and out.

All except one.

Major Chip Hazard.

He bobbed to the surface and floated downstream with the rest of the debris—just in time to avoid being seen by Alan, Archer, and Christy as they stared in amazement at the wreckage of their enemies.

"Um . . . okay if I drive on the way home?" Alan asked.

"Yes!" added Archer quickly.

Christy laughed and handed Alan the keys.

The ride back to the house was very different. Alan, his back straight, his shoulders square with pride, drove the scooter through town at a stately twenty miles an hour, the wind blowing through his hair. Christy sat behind him, her arms around his waist, her cheek against his shoulder.

And on the rear rack sat Archer, the wind washing over him like victory itself.

# CHAPTER
## 17

But if Alan, Christy, and Archer thought it was over, they were wrong. It was only just beginning.

Back at the stream, Chip pulled himself onto a piece of wrecked mega-vehicle. "Old soldiers never die," he said slowly, his belt light flickering. "They just . . ." The wreckage came to a rest at the stream bank. Chip looked up and saw something. Something that seemed to fill the whole night sky.

It was another Chip Hazard.

A giant Chip Hazard. *How could there be another Chip Hazard?* the Major asked himself. How was he to know that part of Heartland Play System's promotional gimmickry for their new toy line was a series of giant balloons floating above every Toy World store across America?

He couldn't know it. But seeing that giant image of himself was like seeing a vision. It gave him hope. It gave him courage. It gave him the strength to climb out of the water, stand up straight, and get ready to go back into action.

"We have lost the battle," said Chip to himself as he scrambled up the embankment. "We will not lose the war."

Alan, Christy, and Archer returned to Alan's house to find a crowd of angry parents standing outside waiting for them. Phil, Stuart, Irene, Marion—and little Tim.

"Uh-oh," said Alan.

"Alan, where have you *been*?" demanded his father.

"Christy, are you all right? Did he hurt you?" Phil asked.

"We need to take a second here," said Irene. "Gain some perspective, find out what happened."

"I *know* what happened," said Phil. "Your son tied up my son, kidnapped my daughter, and drugged me and my wife! Marion is still tripping!"

They all looked at Marion. She *did* look a little out

of it. Indeed, only the fact that Tim was holding her hand kept her upright.

"No, I'm fine," said Marion. "Really. Really fine."

"Not to mention the damage to my house and my garage," said Phil.

Marion spoke up. "Don't forget—the Martians." And she pointed to a tiny group of plastic monsters huddled on Alan's porch, each trying to hide behind another.

"Alan, I found more of those dolls in your room," said Irene.

"And they've been talking to us," added Stuart.

The Gorgonites began apologizing profusely.

"My fault," said Freakenstein.

At the precise moment this confrontation was going on, Joe was retrieving the boxes of Commandos and Gorgonites from Toy World.

"I think that's all of Friday's delivery," said the supervisor. "How come they wanted it back?"

Joe shook his head. "You know the clowns that make the decisions," he said, and got back in the truck.

Five minutes later he had a better idea why the toys were being recalled.

Because a Small Soldier was sitting on his shoulder, holding a steak knife to his throat.

"You've been drafted," said Chip Hazard.

● ● ●

Alan and Christy had just finished telling their story.

There was a long pause. The two kids looked from one adult face to another. Was anyone going to believe them? They scarcely dared to breathe.

At last Stuart opened his mouth. "Alan," he said, and paused. Then he took a deep breath and began again. "I believe you."

"Me too," said Irene. "Thank goodness! We were so worried!"

"Is this entire household insane?" yelled Phil, jumping to his feet. "He says that toys came to life! What's next—the blue fairy drops by with a talking cricket?"

"Dad," said Christy, "he's telling the truth."

"He's brainwashed you, hasn't he?" said Phil. "Don't worry, honey, we'll get you the best deprogrammer money can buy." He shook his head sadly—and looked right into Slamfist's face.

"You can't change programming," said Slamfist.

"See, I told you!" said Alan. "They were hiding—that's what they do!"

"That's it!" said Phil, gathering his family together. He hauled open the door to find Larry Benson and Irwin Wayfair standing outside.

"We're from Heartland Play Systems Consumer Satisfaction," said Irwin. "We're looking for Alan Abernathy."

# CHAPTER
## 18

"There was a problem with the Commandos," said Alan.

"Oh really?" said Larry obnoxiously. "What problem? Bear in mind you may be called to substantiate your claim in a court of law."

That's when Stuart lost it. He slammed his fist into Larry's jaw and knocked him flat on his back.

"Stuart!" said Irene. He spun around toward her.

"Don't say to calm down," he said. "This is the best I've felt in months!"

"I was going to say hit him again," said Irene.

A small figure peered out. "Hey, look, Larry!" said

Irwin in amazement. "It's Archer!"

"Greetings. I am Archer," said Archer. "Who are you?"

"I'm Irwin, I designed you!" said Irwin excitedly. "And all of the Gorgonites. You're all here!"

"We all have to be somewhere," said Archer.

"Making declarative sentences, formulating inquiries, this is incredible!" said Irwin. "You're *alive.*"

Suddenly all the lights went out. Alan peered out the window. "Oh no," he said.

"More Commandos?" asked Christy.

"A lot more," replied Alan.

Joe's truck was parked outside, with dozens of Commando Elite soldiers pouring out of it.

"Hey, where'd they get one of our trucks?" asked Irwin.

A glimpse inside the cab would have told him. Joe was tied to his own steering wheel. He tried in vain to reach, with his teeth, the rope that operated the horn.

Chip's vehicle came wheeling around the side of the house.

Phil threw open the front door, holding a white flag. "Hi, I'm Phil Fimple," he said. "I come to negotiate the surrender of the, uh, Gorgonzolas."

"There will be no surrender!" Chip thundered.

"There will be no mercy! All Gorgonite scum will die!"

The Commandos fired a ball of flame from a barbecue flamethrower. Phil scrambled inside.

"What the heck happened?" he asked.

Larry shook his head. "They've targeted all of us," he said.

"If you're not a Commando . . ." Irwin began.

". . . you're a Gorgonite," Larry finished.

The Commandos began their attack. A tank with a nail gun mounted to it fired a burst of nails into the window, smashing it to smithereens. Another tank started firing flaming tennis balls through the broken window.

The tennis balls bounced wildly around the room, setting small fires wherever they landed. Irene pushed Marion and Tim into the closet and shut the door. But not before she grabbed a tennis racquet from the top shelf. She stripped off the cover and started batting the flaming tennis balls back out the window. They flew through the ranks of the advancing Commandos like—well, like flaming tennis balls.

"There's gotta be a way to stop those things!" Stuart yelled. "We can't keep relying on my wife's net game!"

"The only thing that might work is an electromagnetic pulse," said Irwin as he and Larry struggled to push a heavy curio cabinet in front of a window.

"Then let's make one of those!" shouted Christy, piling sofa cushions against another window.

"Okay!" Larry said sarcastically. "All we need is a nuclear warhead."

There was a pause.

"Actually, any electrical device generates an electromagnetic field," Phil remarked. "Just not a very big one."

The sofa cushions exploded in a burst of feathers as another Commando missile crashed into the room. "We're going to need a big one," Alan said.

Outside, the Commandos attached a bunch of spray cans to the back fence, lit the fuse, and stood back as a large chunk of fence crashed into the backyard. More Commandos came pouring through the breach in the fence.

"They're in the backyard!" shouted Alan. Suddenly he had an inspiration. "There's a power pole back there. There are two huge transformers on it! Could we use those to make an electro-whatever?"

"If we could blow them up, it'd work!" said Irwin.

"Don't suppose you have any dynamite," said Larry.

Phil spoke up. "You could connect the transformers together!"

"Right!" crowed Irwin. "We just have to create a circuit, and they'll cross-phase!"

Since the Commandos had cut the power to Alan's house, and there had to be power running through the transformers to make them overload, Christy, Irwin, and Larry would have to make their way over to the Fimple house to turn on everything inside. Larry was scared.

"I'm not going out there!" he cried.

Irwin gazed at him levelly. "Larry—we have to."

"I hate you, Irwin," said Larry. But he knew his co-worker was right. The three quietly slipped outside.

In the kitchen Alan had found what he was looking for—a pipe wrench and a pair of rubber gloves.

Stuart discovered what his son was doing and started yelling. "Alan, whatever you're thinking, forget it! You're not going out there!"

"Dad, there's no time. I've got to—"

"It's too dangerous," his father said.

Alan shook his head. "We've only got one chance at this."

Stuart was insistent. "I'm responsible for you, and I'm not going to let you . . ."

Alan cut him off. "Dad. We have no choice." He looked his father in the eye. "You've got to trust me."

Stuart paused. This was a side to his son he had never seen before. A brave one. A determined one. He sighed. "Alan, put on your coat."

As they left the room, one of the kitchen cabinets creaked open and a small head peeked out.

It was Archer, watching them go.

# CHAPTER
## 19

Stuart burst out of the sun porch swinging a broom wildly, smacking Commandos left and right. He made his way to the flamethrower, which pivoted to target him. Stuart shoved the wooden end of the broom into the barrel and dove aside. The tank exploded.

Alan ran down the steps. "All right, Dad!" he said. The next thing they knew, a nail-gun tank came after them, hitting Stuart in the leg. Alan and Stuart scrambled desperately back to the sun porch and got there just in time.

From the shelter of the porch, Alan raised his head

to look out over the backyard. The electricity pole seemed impossibly far away. How was he ever going to make it?

● ━ ● ━ ●

In Alan's kitchen, Archer stood tall—addressing apparently empty air.

"Gorgonites," he said, "we must help Alan!"

There was a long pause—and then the Gorgonites began to appear. Punch-It and Scratch-It emerged from the oven, Insaniac from a shelf, Slamfist and Freakenstein from a cabinet, and Ocula from the cutlery drawer.

"But if we fight," said Slamfist, "we will lose."

"If we hide, we will *still* lose," said Archer.

Archer held out his hand, palm down. "No more hiding," he said. Punch-It put his hand on top of Archer's first. Then Insaniac. Slamfist added his boulder, Freakenstein his foot. And finally, Ocula put his eyeball on top.

Archer nodded, satisfied. They'd made their choice.

● ━ ● ━ ●

In the Fimple living room, Christy, Irwin, and Larry were rushing around, switching on every light and lamp and electrical device they could see.

"The fuse box is in the front closet!" shouted Christy.

But even as she spoke, a saw-blade tank was sawing its way through the front leg of the china cabinet. Without warning, it toppled over. Irwin pushed Larry and Christy out of the way. But there was no time to save himself. The huge cabinet smashed down on top of him.

The saw-blade tank ran right over Larry's arm. As he screamed in pain, Christy picked it up and threw it out the window.

"I'm okay!" said Larry. "Let's help Irwin." He and Christy struggled to lift the heavy piece of furniture off him.

Irwin opened his eyes slowly. "We gotta get to the fuse box!" he said. "Turn on every piece of electronic equipment you've got in this place!" And he jumped to his feet and threw himself back into the fray.

Alan and Stuart were still trapped next to the sun porch. There were just too many Commandos, too many tanks, too many missiles.

And then, against all hope, Punch-It dropped in front of the nail gun, a slingshot stretched between his horns. Scratch-It pulled back and released a rock, scoring a bull's-eye on the driver of the nail-firing tank and knocking him out of his seat. Insaniac gave a crazy scream of laughter and spun around faster and faster, hitting every Commando in his path.

Slamfist swung his boulder, taking out a group of Small Soldiers. Ocula wrapped his eye-stalk around a Commando's neck like an anaconda—and off popped his head. Freakenstein turned the nail-gun tank on the Commandos. It was time for a taste of their own medicine.

"Alan," said Archer, tugging on his sleeve, "you may go now."

"Archer, listen," said Alan. "When that thing explodes you guys are gonna be fried, just like the Commandos." He felt terrible saying this, but he couldn't lie to his friend. And that was how he thought of Archer now—as his friend.

Archer pointed to the pole. "Go," he said.

Alan took a deep breath and sprinted across the backyard. He reached the pole, tucked the wrench into his waistband, and started to climb. He reached the cross spar at the top, looped a rubber hose around his waist to secure himself, and was just about to reach up to put the pipe wrench in place between the transformers—when Chip's helicopter zoomed in from the direction of the house, firing as it came.

Before Alan knew what was happening, two bottle rockets had exploded on either side of him, his precious wrench had dropped out of his hand and he himself had fallen halfway down the pole. The garden hose stopped him with a jerk, catching him under his armpits. But he was stuck, his arms forced over his head, a perfect target as Chip brought the chopper in for another run.

In the Fimple's dark front closet, Irwin frantically tore at the metal facing of the fuse box, trying to get at the wires. Suddenly the lights in the entryway went out. Irwin reached up to snap the circuit back on, but the box cover fell and banged him in the head. Larry reached in and lifted it for him. "Don't let the main breaker close," said Irwin, and continued to yank at the wires.

Insaniac swung the nail gun around to hit the chopper and help Alan, but it wouldn't tilt up far enough. And then, magically, it did! Archer and Freakenstein were lifting up the tank.

Insaniac fired, hit, and sent the chopper spiraling out of control.

But not before Chip had leapt to safety on top of the pole.

Alan wriggled desperately as Chip climbed down toward him, trying to get some footing, but the pole was too slippery. Any minute now, Alan knew, he'd go crashing helplessly to the ground. Chip pulled a razor-blade knife from behind his back. "Expect no mercy," he snarled.

Down on the ground, Archer grabbed his cross-bow, fitted a nail into his bow, attached some fishing line, and shot it into the air. It soared over the power line and plunged down. Insaniac caught the nail in his teeth and began to spin like a whirling dervish, hauling Archer straight up to the power pole. "Major Chip Hazard!" he shouted.

"Gorgonite scum!" growled Chip, and swiped at Archer with the blade. Archer deflected the blow with his crossbow. Chip stabbed Archer's hand, and Archer went hurtling to the ground.

"Victory is ours!" said Chip in triumph.

"Shut up, you stupid toy!" Alan shouted. Archer had given him the precious seconds he needed to wriggle out of the hose and regain his footing. As Alan saw his friend lying flat on the ground far below him, he was furious. He didn't have a wrench to fuse the two transformers? Never mind—he had something even better. He grabbed Chip and jammed *him* between the two transformers.

White-hot sparks flew as Chip struggled in vain to free himself—and Alan crashed to the ground and lay there, the wind knocked out of him. He raised his head and saw a sea of Commandos pouring across the lawn toward him.

Suddenly Christy roared up on a stripped-down lawn tractor. "C'mon!" she yelled. "Is this going to become a pattern for our relationship?"

"Relationship?" said Alan, scrambling aboard.

Christy headed for the gap in the fence—while up on the transformer, electricity pouring through him, Chip began to melt.

In the last seconds before the transformers connected with each other, his metal skeleton showed clearly through the plastic—and then he disappeared forever, in a massive burst of power.

The Electromagnetic Pulse.

The pulse rolled out from the pole like a ripple spreading across a pond.

The lawn tractor died, continuing to roll forward only because of its own momentum. A Commando vehicle, out of control, crashed into the side of Christy's house.

The wave pulsed out through the neighborhood, plunging house after house into darkness. In the Fimple and Abernathy backyards the Commandos went into death throes, melting down, exploding, spinning in place, heads flying off.

It was a dance of death.

Stuart threw his arms around Alan and Christy.

"You are—that was—incredible," he said.

Irene ran outside and embraced Alan. "My baby!" she cried. "You're all right."

"Mom!" said Alan, embarrassed. And then looked over to see Christy being given the same treatment by *her* parents. Each caught the other's eye and grinned self-consciously.

Larry looked at Irwin, and Irwin looked at Larry. Then Larry threw one arm around Irwin's neck in a hug. With the other, he gave him a noogie.

# CHAPTER
## 20

An hour later people in white containment suits swarmed all over the Abernathy and Fimple properties, armed with tongs and hazardous-waste disposal bags. Ms. Kegel was in charge, talking to the policemen and the firemen. Finally she pulled out a cell phone. "The area is secure," she said. "Bring him down."

Out of the morning sky an executive helicopter descended toward the street. The door opened and Gil Mars stepped out and strode toward the wrecked houses, his feet crunching over smashed Commandos. Ms. Kegel ran up to meet him. "Sir, we're almost through here," she said. "There's just the matter of some . . . compensation for the involved parties."

Mars spotted Joe, standing by his truck. "You. You work for us, don't you?" Joe nodded. "Would you mind doing me a tremendous favor and getting your truck with the giant Globotech logo out of here?" Mars asked. "Before the news crews show up!"

Joe stared at him. "I don't know, Mr. Mars," he said. "I might have some trouble working the gears . . . what with the crippling head injury and emotional distress I've recently suffered."

Mars nodded to Ms. Kegel, who hit some keys on her imprinter. A check was spit out, and she handed it to Joe. His eyes widened. "Yes, sir, right away," he said, as his fingers closed around the biggest check he'd ever seen in his life. He turned to Alan. "Keep your nose clean, kid."

"I'll try," said Alan. "Sorry Joe."

Joe headed for his truck. "Forget it. Toys is hell."

Phil stepped up to Gil Mars. "Oh, you're not off the hook yet," he said. "There's just the little matter of some massive damage to my home! And my garage. And my audio-visual component system! And—"

Ms. Kegel printed another check. She handed it to

Mars, who handed it to Phil. He looked at it and swallowed.

"And . . . this is . . . good," Phil said.

"What about *our* house?" asked Irene.

"And what about the pain and anguish and humiliation!" added Stuart. "I'm not sure even *you* have enough money to pay for that!"

Ms. Kegel did the check routine again.

Stuart gaped. "Okay," he admitted. "Maybe you do."

Irene took a look. "He does," she said.

Larry and Irwin looked at each other and walked up to the man they were certain was just about to fire them. Larry spoke first. He looked ready to grovel. "Um, sir, I just wanted to assure you that I . . ." He paused for a moment and looked at Irwin. In the old days Larry would have pointed the finger straight at his partner. But now—things were different. ". . . take full responsibility for this," continued Larry. "It was all my idea to put in the chips," he said, knowing his career as a toy designer was over. He braced himself for Mars's anger.

"Yeah?" said Mars. "Well, you made a big mistake." Then he bent down and picked something up. It was Chip Hazard's decapitated head.

"What was the asking price on these things?" he asked.

"Um. One hundred nineteen dollars," replied Larry.

"Have your people stick a couple more zeros at the end of that number," Mars said. He turned to Irwin. "And you start designing some new packaging."

"Sir?" asked Irwin, puzzled.

Mars grinned. "I know some South American rebels who might find these toys very . . . entertaining."

As the three men took off in the corporate helicopter, Mars looked down and surveyed the yard, the devastation. He sighed. "You know, this would have made one heck of a commercial."

"Yeah, incredible," said Irwin.

"Probably sell a lot of toys," added Larry.

Down in the backyard, Phil watched the chopper depart. Tim was in his arms, half asleep.

"Dad?" said Tim sleepily. "You know my birthday?"

"Uh-huh?" said Phil.

"I just want clothes," said Tim. And he fell asleep again.

Christy spotted Alan, who was searching through the bushes.

"Did you find Archer?" she asked.

Alan shook his head sadly. "No, none of them."

They looked at each other dejectedly. "I better go," Christy said. "See you later?"

"Yeah, okay," said Alan.

Without a word Christy leaned forward and gave Alan a light kiss on the cheek. Emboldened, Alan grabbed her wrist, pulled her close, and gave her a kiss. A *real* kiss.

Alan stood in the backyard, throwing dead Commandos into a pile. He wasn't thinking about what he was doing, he wasn't even thinking about Archer and the Gorgonites. He just felt numb.

Then he heard an odd sound. *Ding, ding, ding.*

He listened, more closely. *Ding, ding, ding.*

It was coming from underneath an upside-down satellite dish. The satellite dish that Stuart and Phil had almost come to blows over. Curious, Alan hooked his fingers under the edge of the dish and lifted.

Underneath were the Gorgonites, twitching, stuck in endless loops of repetitive motion.

"Archer!" Alan cried, hoping against hope. "Are you okay?" He held his breath.

"Greetings, I am Archer, emissary of the Gorgonites," Archer said in a mechanical voice.

Alan's face fell. "Oh man, your chip got fried. Just like all the Commandos'."

"The Commandos are dead?" Archer asked. He turned to the others. "Gorgonites! We won!"

The Gorgonites all came to life, laughing and cheering.

"I knew we would," said Freakenstein.

"Archer, I'm glad you made it," Alan said to his friend.

"I'm glad *you* made it Alan," replied Archer.

"I guess the dish must have shielded you," Alan mused. "Pretty smart."

"We did what we do best," Archer said. "We hid."

Slowly, as all the tension of the night flowed out of him, Alan began to laugh.

And for the first time—so did Archer.

# CHAPTER
## 21

It was a bright, sunny day. Alan knelt on the river-bank, next to one of Stuart's wooden boats. The boat was loaded with Gorgonites.

"You're sure you want to do this?" said Alan.

"Yes, Alan," said Archer. "It is time for us to go."

Alan nodded. "I understand," he said. "But where?"

"We're going home," Archer said solemnly.

Alan was confused. "The Land of Gorgon?" he said. "But Archer, there is no . . . "

Archer broke in. "Alan, even if you can't see something, it doesn't mean it isn't there."

Alan stood up and pushed the boat into the water.

The wind picked up, and the white sail billowed out. The Gorgonites all waved good-bye.

"Farewell Alan," they called. "Good-bye! We'll miss you!"

As the boat moved away downstream, Alan stood there, watching it dwindle into an almost invisible speck in the brightness of the river.

And then Archer was gone.

Several days later, far along the river, a tiny craft appeared out of a thick layer of mist. Aboard it was a group of strange plastic figures. The mist turned to moisture and ran down their bodies like condensation on a window.

Ocula, acting as the lookout, began squeaking excitedly. The other Gorgonites gathered around, looking at a picture on a torn piece of cardboard, and then up at a shape appearing out of the mist ahead of them.

Could it be the place they had been searching for?

The Gorgonites turned the boat toward the mysterious shore.

Another adventure was about to begin.